Emily Eyefinger, Secret Agent

ALSO BY DUNCAN BALL

Emily Eyefinger

Emily Eyefinger, Secret Agent

Duncan Ball
Drawings by George Ulrich

HALF MOON BOOKS
Published by Simon & Schuster
New York   London   Toronto   Sydney   Tokyo   Singapore

HALF MOON BOOKS
Published by Simon & Schuster
1230 Avenue of the Americas, New York, New York 10020
Text copyright © 1993 by Duncan Ball
Illustrations copyright © 1993 by George Ulrich
All rights reserved including the right of reproduction
in whole or in part in any form.
HALF MOON BOOKS is a trademark of Simon & Schuster.
Also available in a SIMON & SCHUSTER BOOKS FOR YOUNG READERS hardcover edition.
First Half Moon Books edition, 1994.
Designed by Vicki Kalajian.
The text for this book is set in 16/22 Horley Old Style.
Manufactured in the United States of America

10 9 8 7 6 5 4 3 2

Library of Congress Cataloging-in-Publication Data
Ball, Duncan. Emily Eyefinger, secret agent / by Duncan Ball;
illustrated by George Ulrich.   p.   cm.
Summary: A young girl feels different from everyone else
because she has an eye on the end of one finger, but
it comes in handy on occasion, such as when she is helping to catch a spy.
[1. Eye—Fiction. 2. Spies—Fiction. 3. Identity—Fiction.]
I. Ulrich, George, ill. II. Title   PZ7.B1985En   1993
[Fic]—dc20   92-30518   CIP   ISBN: 0-671-89906-6

Contents

Emily Eyefinger, Secret Agent

1

Emily First Hand

It wasn't easy being the only little girl who had an eye on the end of her finger. It certainly wasn't Emily's fault that she was born that way. It was nobody's fault, really. It just happened.

It's true that Emily had two normal eyes just like everyone else. So she had no problem seeing. And it's also true that having the extra eye could be fun. She used it to see around corners and through cracks in the floor or holes in the wall. She could even look behind her when she was walking without turning her head. At school she could face her teacher and still peek out the window with her finger.

When people asked her if she liked having an eye on her finger, she would say, "On the one hand I like it. But on the other hand I don't."

Emily could do many things with her eye-finger. But there were things that everyone else could do but Emily couldn't. Every now and then that made her sad.

One day Emily was watching her parents fix up their bathroom. The work was almost done. Her mother was caulking around the bathtub to keep the water from going down behind.

"I'm sick and tired of my eyefinger," Emily said. "I want the doctor to take it off."

Her father stopped hammering. Her mother stopped caulking.

"You mean get rid of it?" Mr. Eyefinger asked.

"Yes," Emily said, "that's exactly what I mean."

"But I thought you liked it," Mrs. Eyefinger said. "How about your little joke? Remember? 'On the one hand I like it and on the other hand I don't'?"

"It's not funny anymore," Emily said. "The doctor said that he'd take it off if I wanted him to."

"But remember," Mrs. Eyefinger warned, "he can't put it back on again. Once it's gone, it's gone for good."

"That's okay with me," Emily said.

Her parents looked at each other. Emily went to the new basin and started brushing her teeth.

"Emily," her father said, "can we talk about this?"

Emily nodded.

"It's true that sometimes you get dirt in your eye when you're playing. I know that's not much fun."

"And soap in my eye when I wash my

hands," Emily reminded him. "I can close my eyelid but it still gets in."

"But you have that nice plastic bubble to protect it," Mrs. Eyefinger said. "You just have to remember to put it on."

"There are lots and lots of things I still can't do," Emily said. "Daddy won't even let me hammer in nails."

"You might hit your eye," Mr. Eyefinger explained. "That bubble wouldn't protect you from a hammer."

"You said I could have it taken off if I wanted to."

"Of course you can. We just want to make sure you really really want to."

"I really really *really* want to," said Emily.

Emily started brushing her teeth again.

"Is someone picking on you at school?" her mother asked.

"Nope," Emily said (but it sounded more like "oke" because of the toothbrush in her mouth).

"Are people staring at you? You can always put your hand in your pocket," Mr. Eyefinger said. "When you do that you look like any other little girl."

"That's not it," Emily said.

"Think of the wonderful help you've been," Mrs. Eyefinger said. "You rescued that Mousefinder boy when he was stuck down a hole."

"Yes, that was good," Emily admitted.

"And you found that lost snake at the zoo," Mr. Eyefinger said. "You were in the newspaper. You even helped the police catch those robbers."

"Things like that will probably never happen again," said Emily.

"Maybe they will," said Mr. Eyefinger. "You can't tell."

He watched as Emily brushed her teeth some more.

"Look at the way you do that," he said.

"What do you mean?" Emily asked.

"You brush for a while and then you put your eyefinger right in your mouth."

"That way I can see if I've missed anything."

"*We* can't do that," her mother said. "*We* have to look in the mirror and we still can't see the backs of our teeth. No wonder you have the cleanest teeth in the family."

Emily frowned.

"Swimming," she said. And then she said "Swimming swimming swimming!" really loud.

"What about swimming?" Mrs. Eyefinger asked.

"We just started swimming lessons at school. If I stay in the pool more than a minute, water gets in my finger bubble. It makes my eyefinger sting."

"But you often put your finger in Fluffy's bowl to watch him," Mrs. Eyefinger said, referring to Emily's goldfish. "I've seen you do it lots of times."

"That's different. The swimming pool water has chemicals in it."

"I see," her mother said. "Here, I have just the thing. We'll put some of this caulking compound around the edge of your finger bubble. That will keep the water out." Which is exactly what she did. "Is that better?"

"Yes. Now I feel better about my eyefinger," Emily said.

"Now you can swim and see where you're going," Mr. Eyefinger said. "That way you won't bump into the end of the pool."

Emily gave him a big hug.

"On the one hand I like it," she said. "But on the other hand I don't. I guess I'll keep my eyefinger a little bit longer and see what happens."

2

Emily and the Tree That Squeaked

Emily was lying on the couch reading a book called *Sarah Spy, Secret Agent*. The book was about the youngest person ever to join the secret service. Emily was almost at the end of the story. Sarah was following a spy and getting closer and closer to his hideout. Step by step through the dark streets she went. There was danger around every corner. It was so exciting that Emily could hardly stand it. Suddenly there was a knock at

Emily's door. She dropped the book and sat up straight.

"Who is it?" she called.

"Emily, come quickly! There's a tree that's squeaking!"

At the front door were two children who lived nearby. They were Damian and Beth Young and they were both younger than Emily.

"What *are* you talking about?" Emily asked.

"It's squeaking and they're chopping it down!" Damian said. "You've got to make them stop!"

Damian's little sister, Beth, stood next to him with her thumb in her mouth. She had a small piece of blanket pressed to the side of her face. Her big, sad eyes looked up at Emily.

"Who's cutting down the tree?" Emily asked.

"Come with us," Damian said. "We'll show you."

Emily could see in their faces that something was very wrong. She wanted to finish reading her book, but their problem seemed more important.

Around the corner they went. In front of Damian and Beth's house were two workers. A woman was up in a cherry picker cutting off the top branches of a tree with a chainsaw. A man was standing on the ground nearby. Under the tree were piles of branches.

The man stepped forward when he saw the children coming. The noise of the chainsaw was deafening.

"Out of the way, kids!" he shouted. "This is dangerous!"

The children pointed at the tree. They were all talking at once.

"Stay back!" the man yelled. "I'm sorry if you don't want the tree cut down. We have to do it. It's dead. If we don't cut it down it may fall on someone."

"They say they heard it squeaking," Emily yelled.

"What?" the man shouted back.

"It was squeaking!"

"Peaking?"

"No, squeaking!"

"Leaking?"

Emily shook her head.

"Stop for a minute, Vicky," the man yelled. "I want to have a word with the kids."

One more branch came crashing down and then the chainsaw stopped.

"What's this about a leaping tree?" he said.

"It's not leaping, it's squeaking," Damian said. "Listen."

They were all quiet for a minute. Everyone was listening.

"I don't hear a thing," the man said.

"My sister did," Damian said, pointing to Beth. "She heard it squeaking just before you started cutting."

"Is that right, little girl?"

Beth nodded. She didn't say anything. She still had her thumb deep in her mouth.

"Old trees sometimes creak, especially when the wind blows."

"No!" Beth screamed.

"All right, all right. Keep your shirt on, kid. What sort of squeak did it make?"

Beth thought for a minute and then made some squeaking sounds in a tiny voice. "*Eeeeek eeeeek eeeeek*," she said. Then she put her thumb back in her mouth.

"What do you make of that, Vicky?" the man yelled up the tree.

"Beats me," Vicky answered.

"Does your little friend think trees can talk?" the man asked Emily. "Maybe she's got a lively imagination."

Beth narrowed her eyes and gave him her dirtiest look.

"She thinks there's something *inside* the tree," Emily explained. "Something that goes squeak."

"You mean like a bird?" the man said.

"Yes. Just look up there," Emily said,

13

pointing to a hole halfway up the trunk. "There may be a nest in that hole."

Vicky moved the cherry picker down to look in the hole.

"I can't see a thing," she said. "It's too small. I can't get my head in to look down. Anybody in there?" she yelled in the hole.

The man on the ground said, "Okay, kids. Off you go."

"No! No!" Beth yelled at him.

"Sorry, little girl, but we have to finish the job. If there's anything in the hole we'll find it when we cut the tree down. But I don't think there's anything in there."

Little Beth pointed to Emily.

"Why is she doing that?" the man asked Emily.

"She wants me to look in the hole with my eyefinger," Emily explained.

"Your what?"

"You see I . . . er . . . have this . . . er . . ." Emily started to explain. She had her left hand deep in her pocket. "I mean, most people just have fingernails on the ends of their fingers—but not me. I guess you might say that I'm different. Boy, am I different!"

"What *are* you talking about?" the man asked.

"Here, take a look," Emily said, showing him her finger and making the eyelid blink so he'd know it was real.

"Well, darn my socks!" the man said. "Hey, Vicky. Get a load of this! This little girl has an eye on the end of her finger!"

"A what? I don't believe it!"

"It's an eye! A real live eye on her finger! It just blinked at me!"

"You don't say."

"I do say. Come down here."

The woman brought the cherry picker down. She looked closely at Emily's eyefinger while the children giggled.

"Well, I'll be," she said (though she didn't say *what* she'd be).

In a minute Emily had persuaded her to take her up the tree. When she got to the hole, she took her little flashlight out of her pocket. Then she held it and put her hand right inside the tree trunk. There she saw six little furry balls bunched up together.

"Kittens," said Emily. "Little kittens. They've just been born. They're too little even to meow. Their eyes are still closed."

"Can you get them out?" the man asked.

"No, they're much too far down. I can't reach them."

"Well, we can't cut a tree down with kittens in it. But how can we get them out?"

Emily thought for a moment. "Do you know anyone who has a cat that was about to have kittens?" she asked Damian and Beth.

The children shook their heads. Emily looked around and saw a cat hiding under a bush nearby.

"Whose cat is that?" she asked.

"Tiddumtat," Beth said.

"That's our cat," Damian explained. "Beth called her Tiddumtat because she couldn't say kitty cat."

"Maybe they're her kittens," Emily said.

"She was getting a little fat," Damian said. "I thought she needed to go on a diet."

"Let's get out of the way and see what she does," Emily said.

Sure enough, when everyone got away Tiddumtat crept up the tree and into the hole. Then, one by one, she brought out the kittens in her mouth and carried them under the house. When she was finished Emily looked down the hole again to make sure they were all gone.

"It's a good thing you have that eye-thing," Vicky said. "We could have hurt those little kittens. By the way, my name is Vicky Tree-trimmer. My partner and I would like to thank you for your help."

"Did you say your name is Treetrimmer?"

"Yes, it's odd, isn't it. My name's Treetrimmer and my job is trimming trees."

"My name's Eyefinger," Emily said, "and I have an eye on my finger. It's strange how these things happen, isn't it?"

"Names are weird," the woman said. "I heard about a guy named Drinkwater who used to drink lots and lots of water. Life sure is funny sometimes," she added with a laugh.

Emily turned to Beth. "It's a good thing you heard those squeaks," she said. "Are you happy now?"

Beth took her thumb out of her mouth and wiggled her finger at Emily.

"I think she wants to tell you something," Damian said.

When Emily bent down to listen, Beth gave her a big wet kiss on the cheek.

"Well, I guess that answers that," Emily said with a smile. Then she went back home to finish reading *Sarah Spy, Secret Agent*.

3

Emily Acts

Emily's friend Janey Star wanted to be famous. She wanted to be a movie star. She acted in plays at school. Even when she wasn't acting she loved dressing up as different people. Her favorite role was of a rich actress. Janey would put on one of her mother's long dresses and lots of makeup and then lie back on the couch blinking her long false eyelashes.

"Emily daaaarling," she'd say. "Plee-uz tell

my driver to bring my car. They're expecting me at the theatuh at seven."

She also liked being a pirate. Once she put black wax on some of her teeth to make it look as if they were missing. With a scarf around her head, a patch over one eye, a bushy black beard, and a stuffed parrot on her shoulder, she looked pretty scary to Emily.

"Har har har," she said in her deepest voice. "Give me your jewels or die like a dog!"

"Janey, don't do that!" Emily said. "I don't like it."

Janey put her face close to Emily's and opened her eyes wide.

"How dare you speak, you little worm! Give me your jewels or I'll cut off your head!"

"Janey, don't do that! I hate it when you do that. It's too real."

"It is? Then I'm a pretty good actor, huh?"

"You sure are. A bit too good, if you ask me."

"You could be an actor too," Janey said. "We could be in a play together. It would be a lot of fun."

Emily didn't want to act. She never would have acted in anything if it hadn't been for the chicken pox. It wasn't Emily who caught the chicken pox. It was Simon Sickly. And he caught it just before he was about to act in a school play.

The name of the play was *The Clever Little Princess and the Really Dumb Robber*. Janey Star had made up the play. Of course she was going to be the clever little princess. Simon was supposed to be the really dumb robber. The play was part of Parents' Night and everyone was dying to see it.

"Simon is sick," Janey told Emily. "He can't be in the play. Why don't *you* be the robber instead? You could do it, I know you could."

"No, I couldn't," Emily said.

"Why not?"

"Because I don't know anything about acting."

"Don't be silly. Everyone can act. Even I can act."

"That's because you practice all the time. You're really really good at it."

(This was just what Janey wanted to hear.)

"Yes, I suppose you're right," she said.

"Besides," Emily said, "everyone will stare at my eyefinger. They won't listen to a word I say."

"That's just an excuse. You could put your hand in your pocket. Any more excuses?"

"Janey, Parents' Night is tonight! I can't learn all those lines by tonight. No one could do that."

"I'm the one who does most of the talking," Janey said. "But I suppose you're right. Oh, well. I guess we'll just have to cancel the play."

Janey sounded brave but Emily knew that

her friend was sad. She was about to cry. Emily could hear it in her voice. Then Emily thought of something.

"This play is very important to you, isn't it?" she said.

"Yes, it is," Janey answered.

"Then I'll do it. I'll be in the play if you want me to."

"But Emily, how can you? You can't possibly learn all the lines by tonight. You said so yourself."

"I have an idea. I won't have to learn anything."

"Oh, Emily, you're a life saver. I hope you know what you're doing."

"You wait and see."

"Oh, one thing. Promise me you won't be late. You're always late for everything."

"I promise."

That night, all the parents came to Parents' Night. Mr. and Mrs. Eyefinger sat in the front row next to Janey's parents. The school principal made a speech and then there were a lot of songs. Finally it was time for *The Clever Little Princess and the Really Dumb Robber.*

Janey and Emily were behind the curtain. Janey looked beautiful in her silver gown and long blond wig. On top of her head was a crown made out of a cereal box wrapped with foil.

Janey had dressed Emily up to look like a robber. She gave her a black mask that went around her eyes and a striped sweater. Then Emily put on a long coat.

"What's that for?" Janey whispered.

"Watch," Emily said.

Emily quickly studied the pieces of paper that had her lines written on them. Then she put them in the pocket of her coat along with her tiny flashlight.

"I get it!" Janey said. "You can read your lines right in your pocket! You don't have to remember them. What a great idea! Okay, now I go out first and you come in when the lights dim. Got it?"

"I guess so," said Emily, "but I have butterflies in my stomach—and they're as big as birds."

"So do I," Janey admitted. "That's normal. Even really super famous actors get scared when they act. Take some slow deep breaths. That helps."

Everything went perfectly. Janey sat on her throne and gave a wonderful speech. She said that someone was breaking into the palace and stealing things. No one could catch the robber, not even the palace guards. She said that *she* was going to catch the robber because *she* was a clever little princess.

Janey pretended to fall asleep on her throne. Then the lights went dim and Emily came climbing in the window. She crept around stealing things and putting them in a big bag. She took all the silverware and she even found some money under the princess's

bed and stole that. Then she reached for Janey's crown.

"Not so fast!" Janey yelled, waking up and grabbing the crown.

Emily let go and jumped back. She put her hand in her pocket and turned on the flashlight. She started reading her lines.

"Give me that crown, princess," Emily said. "I'm a robber and I'll beat you up if you don't."

"Oh, you are *really* dumb!" Janey said. "Can't you see that I'm not a princess?"

"You're not?"

"No, I'm your fairy godmother."

"My what?" Emily asked. "I didn't know I had one of those."

"Well, that just shows how dumb you are," Janey said, and everyone in the audience laughed. "I can grant you any wish you want."

"You can?"

"Of course. That's what fairy godmothers do. That's pretty much all they *can* do."

"Hang on a minute," Emily said. "If you're my fairy godmother, where's your wand? You're supposed to tap me on the head with your wand. Then I make a wish and turn around three times."

"Don't be silly. We don't use wands anymore," Janey said. "They're out of fashion. We use magic ropes now."

"Magic ropes?"

Janey took out a long piece of rope. "Hold one end in your hand and make a wish. Don't tell me what it is. Then turn around ten times."

Emily pretended that she was thinking for a minute and then she took the rope and started turning around.

"Ten times?" she asked.

"Ten times," Janey said.

The rope went around and around Emily's middle and her arms were stuck under it. Finally she stopped and Janey tied a big knot so Emily couldn't move.

Some people in the audience giggled.

"Now do I get my wish?" Emily asked.

"No, but I get mine. You're going straight to prison! You are the dumbest robber I have ever met."

"Hey, you tricked me!" Emily yelled and everyone roared with laughter.

Janey turned to the audience and said, "And so ends the story of *The Clever Little Princess and the Really Dumb Robber*."

Everyone laughed again and started clapping. Emily and Janey bowed as deeply as they could without falling over.

"Now wasn't that fun?" Janey squealed as the curtain came down. "And you got all your lines right. You saved the show. You were really great!"

"Don't thank me, thank my little friend," Emily said, pointing her eyefinger at Janey. "But please don't ask me to do it again. Acting is too scary!"

4

Emily's Expedition

One day Emily got a postcard with a picture of a mouse on it. On the back was a message that said:

Dear Emily,

How are you? I'm fine, thanks. Would you and your mother and father like to come on an ~~egs~~ an ~~exx~~ an ~~eshped~~ an ~~expidish~~ a trip with me and my dad? We're going to look for a very rare kind of mouse. (So what's new?) We will be going to Rodent River. Ever heard of it?

Me neither. Anyway, we'll have lots and lots of fun if we don't get lost. (Hope we don't get lost!) How about it?

Your friend,
Malcolm Mousefinder

Emily ran to her parents. She had gotten a few letters from Malcolm since she helped to rescue him. He usually sent them from far-away places. He went on lots of mousehunting expeditions with his father, Professor Mousefinder. They seemed to have plenty of fun, when they weren't lost. But they almost *always* got lost.

"Oh, please," Emily begged her parents, "can we go?"

"I don't know, dear," Mr. Eyefinger said. "I have a letter from the professor and he says that we'll have to do a lot of horseback riding. Are you sure you can do it?"

"I love horseback riding," Emily said. "I'm sure I can do it for as long as Malcolm can."

"The professor is a very intelligent man," Emily's mother said, "but he does manage to get lost quite often. He and Malcolm spend more time trying to get unlost than they do hunting mice. Sometimes I think he *likes* getting lost."

"Maybe he has trouble reading maps," Emily said. "We can help him."

"You've got a point," Mrs. Eyefinger said. "Okay, let's go with them. It will be a good vacation."

Rodent River was a long way away. On the first day the Eyefingers and the Mousefinders rode on a train and then rented a car and drove over bumpy roads. The next day they rode horses into rocky hills. Everyone's bottom was sore, but they were all having a good time. Then Emily noticed they were riding in circles.

"Excuse me," she said, "but I recognize that rock."

"You mean you've seen it before?" Professor Mousefinder asked.

"Three times," said Emily. "Is it possible we're lost?"

"Possible?" sighed Malcolm. "Are you kidding? We *always* get lost."

"Let's look at a map," Mrs. Eyefinger suggested.

"Map?" Professor Mousefinder said. "I never use those things. Getting lost is half the fun of mousehunting."

"Hmm," Mrs. Eyefinger said. "I wonder what the other half is."

"Finding mice, of course," the professor said. He had a big smile on his face.

Fortunately, Mrs. Eyefinger had thought of everything. She had brought a map and a compass as well. All three Eyefingers and two Mousefinders looked at the map.

"Rodent River is that way," Mrs. Eyefinger said, pointing.

Off they went and, sure enough, just at sunset they came to a river.

"Rodent River at last!" said Professor Mousefinder.

"Goodness! It's very wide," said Emily. "How will we ever get across?"

"We won't," said the professor. "We're going to paddle down it in a rubber raft. But tonight we'll camp here."

That night when the tents were pitched and they were sitting by their campfire eating, Professor Mousefinder told everyone about the mice that he and Malcolm were looking for.

"I'm not sure there are any of them left," said the professor. "They may have died out. No mouseologist — that's a mouse expert like me — has ever seen one."

"How do you know about them?" Emily asked.

"A long time ago people lived along this river. They had many stories about the animals who lived here. Some of these stories were written on animal skins and are in museums. There's one about a mouse with white stripes. The people called them the Mice of the Up and Down Water."

"The Mice of the Up and Down Water," said Emily. "What a strange name. It's so mysterious."

"Yes, it is," Mrs. Eyefinger said. "Water isn't up and down except when it rains. Mostly it's side to side as in rivers and lakes and oceans."

"We don't understand the name," said Professor Mousefinder. "Maybe they thought the stripes looked like water going up and down. I just hope we can find one. Let's get some sleep and we'll paddle down to Rodent Gorge in the morning."

Malcolm had been quiet all day. Even when they were all sitting on a log eating dinner, he didn't say a word. He just peered around in the dark. When he and Emily were in their tent, he finally said, "Can I tell you a secret?"

"Sure," Emily said. "What is it?"

"I'm scared."

"Scared of what?" Emily asked.

"Bears, mainly."

"There aren't any bears out here," Emily said, snuggling down into her sleeping bag. "Go to sleep. Your dad said that you fall asleep in a second."

"Not when I start thinking about bears — and I'm thinking about bears right now. I'm going to be awake all night."

"Don't be silly."

"Uh oh," Malcolm whispered. "Listen to that."

Emily listened. The water rushing down the river was loud but she heard another noise.

"It's a bear! I just know it is!" Malcolm said.

"I'll peek out and see," Emily said.

"Don't do that! It'll attack you if you put your head out."

"Who said anything about putting my head out?"

Emily poked her eyefinger through the tent flap and looked around in the darkness. When her eye got used to the dark, she saw two big yellow eyes staring right back at her. *Hoo hoo hoo* came the noise again. Emily pulled her finger back inside the tent.

"What is it?" Malcolm squealed.

"I'll give you one guess," Emily said.

"A bear!" said Malcolm.

"Is that your guess?"

"Stop it, Emily! Just tell me!"

"It's an owl, silly. What else goes *hoo hoo hoo*?"

"Thank goodness for that," said Malcolm. "And thank goodness for your eyefinger. I wish I had one."

"So now are you going to stop worrying and get some sleep?" Emily asked.

Malcolm didn't answer. He was already sound asleep.

5

Emily Eyefinger,
Mouseologist

The next day Mr. and Mrs. Eyefinger and the Mousefinders put their life jackets on and piled into the big rubber raft. But Emily was still sitting on a rock with her hand in the water.

"Emily, what are you doing?" her father asked.

"There's a whole school of little fish down there," Emily said. "Can't I watch them just a little longer?"

"No, you can't," her mother said. "Now

hurry up. You're going to make us all late."

"It's not fair," said Emily, but she climbed into the raft and helped to push it out into the river.

Soon the water got rough and the raft went faster. Everyone had to hang on to the sides so they wouldn't be thrown out. The trees on the riverbanks raced by and Emily had a tickling feeling in her stomach. Professor Mousefinder was grinning, but Emily could tell that her parents were nervous.

"How will we know when we get to Rodent Gorge?" she asked Professor Mousefinder.

"Don't worry, I'll recognize it. Hang on tight!"

They shot along going faster and faster and bumped up and down. Water sprayed all over them. Finally the rapids ended and the raft slowed down.

"Thank goodness we got through that," Mrs. Eyefinger said. "Those rapids were too rapid for me."

They heard a strange noise up ahead getting louder and louder.

"Excuse me, professor," Mr. Eyefinger said. "But what's all that roaring?"

"I'm not really sure," Professor Mousefinder said as he studied the Eyefingers's map.

Mr. Eyefinger tried to stand up to see but the water was still too rough and he nearly fell out of the raft.

Emily had an idea.

"Grab my legs!" she said.

Emily's parents held one leg and Malcolm and his father held the other one. Together they lifted her up as high as they could.

"What do you see?" Malcolm asked.

"I don't know. The water sort of disappears."

Emily raised her left hand high over her head, shut her eyes, and looked through her eyefinger. Suddenly it got very windy.

"It's a waterfall!" she screamed, but the noise and the wind made it hard to hear.

"Shopping mall?" her mother screamed back. "Did you say there was a shopping mall? Thank goodness!"

"No! Let me down. Paddle to the river-bank! Hurry!"

As soon as they put her down, everyone paddled furiously toward shore. After a few frantic moments they got there—and just in time. Straight ahead was the top of the waterfall.

"We almost went over," Mrs. Eyefinger sighed. "We would have been killed! Thank goodness for Emily's eyefinger."

"That was too close for comfort," Malcolm said. "I'm not going out in that raft again."

"We don't have to," said the professor. "We're here. This is it, Rodent Gorge. I'd recognize that waterfall anywhere."

While Malcolm and his father looked for signs of mice, Emily and her parents walked around the gorge taking photos of the waterfall. They couldn't believe how beautiful it was.

"I've never seen anything like it," Emily said. "The water looks like a big blue piece of glass. It's a glass wall made out of water. And when it hits the bottom, there's a rainbow in the mist."

When they got back they found the professor looking glum.

"I'm afraid it's all been a wild goose chase," he said.

"More like a wild mouse chase, if you ask me," Malcolm said.

"You mean there aren't any mice?" Emily asked.

"Not a one," said Professor Mousefinder. "Not even common ordinary mice. There should be holes in the ground or in trees or something. Malcolm and I haven't even seen a mouse footprint. I'm afraid we've come all this way for nothing."

As they were getting ready for the long

walk back up the river, Emily had one of her bright ideas. She took off her shoes and waded into the river.

"Emily! Where are you going?" Malcolm shouted.

Emily was up to her waist in water, walking closer and closer to the waterfall. She stuck her eyefinger hand straight out and through the waterfall. There, right in front of her eye, was a hole in the rocky cliff. And looking out of the hole was a mouse with white stripes.

"I've found one!" Emily called back to the others. "They must all live behind the waterfall."

"Good job," said Professor Mousefinder. He gave Emily a trap to put behind the waterfall.

"It's better if you do it," he said. "You can see what you're doing."

Soon Emily had caught a tiny striped mouse.

"What a little cutey pooty," she said. "It was worth the whole trip just to see him. What are you going to do with him now?"

"What we always do," said Malcolm. "We'll weigh him and we'll measure him, we'll take his picture, and then we'll let him go back to his family."

When Malcolm and the professor finished their work, they put the tiny mouse on the ground. He jumped into the river and swam right back under the waterfall.

"I'm going to write an article for the *International Journal of Mouseology*," Professor Mousefinder said, "and tell about finding the Mice of the Up and Down Water. And of course I'll mention that wonderful mouse-finding finger of yours, Emily. We never would have found the mouse without you."

"I'm always happy to help," said Emily.

"But I still don't understand the name," said the professor. "Those stripes don't look anything like water to me, up and down *or* sideways."

"Oh, that's easy," said Emily. "That's how I knew where to find him. You see, Up and Down Water must have been another name for a waterfall. It's like a wall. It goes up and down. The people who lived here called them the Mice of the Up and Down Water because they live behind the waterfall."

"Emily, that's brilliant!" Professor Mousefinder said. "When I write my article I'll put your name on it too. From now on you'll be known as Emily Eyefinger, Mouseologist!"

"Well thank you very much, professor, but I think I just want to be Emily Eyefinger, a lucky girl who was born with an eye on the end of her finger."

6

Emily's Frenemy

The telephone rang.

"Emily Bemily, guess what?"

Emily knew that there was only one person who called her "Emily Bemily."

"I can't guess, Wilbur," she said.

"You're not the only person in the world with an eye on their finger," Wilbur said. "I saw a man with one too."

"Are you sure?"

"Yes. I saw his show."

"What *are* you talking about? What kind of show?"

"Magnificent Marvin's Super Spectacular Magic Show. He came to our school today. He's going to be at your school tomorrow. He talks about his eyefinger and shows everybody that it's real! He's great!"

Emily knew there was going to be a magic show at school, but no one had told her that the magician had an eye on his finger. She thought about it all afternoon.

"Finally there's someone else like me!" she told her father. "I want to meet him. I want to talk about our eyefingers. He can be a real friend!"

"I wouldn't get my hopes up if I were you," Mr. Eyefinger said. "What if it's only a trick? It is a magic show, after all. Magic shows are full of tricks."

"Oh, Dad," Emily said. "I'm sure it's not a trick. It's just got to be real."

The next morning everyone on the school

bus was talking about Magnificent Marvin's Super Spectacular Magic Show. None of them talked about his eyefinger. Emily was the only one who knew about it and she didn't tell anyone.

After recess it was time for the show. Terry Meaney wanted the class to watch him make a coin disappear, but everyone was running around the classroom, doing their own tricks. Emily's teacher, Ms. Plump (who was a little on the chubby side), asked the class to make a neat line and walk quietly to the auditorium. Emily sat next to Janey Star.

Magnificent Marvin did the most wonderful tricks. He pulled rabbits out of a box and pigeons out of handkerchiefs. Emily looked for his eyefinger but she couldn't see anything. He had thick gloves on. One of the gloves had a shiny part at the tip, but Emily was too far away to see what it was.

"Who wants to know how I do my tricks?" the magician asked.

Everyone yelled, "We do."

"I'm sorry, I can't hear you," the man said, putting his hand behind his ear.

"WE DO!" the children yelled even louder.

"Okay," the magician said, "you don't have to shout, I'm not deaf. My tricks are very easy to do because there's something special about my hand. Can anyone guess what it is?" Everyone was quiet. "I have an eye on the end of my finger," the man said.

Some of the children giggled and they all looked at Emily. Marvin didn't notice this. He just pointed the finger with the shiny tip around the room.

"Under that piece of glass is a tiny eye. I was born with it. Believe me, when you have an eye on your finger there are lots of tricks you can do. But I see you don't believe me."

With this, Marvin tied a black blindfold around his eyes. He pointed the shiny finger of his glove at the audience and said, "Okay, somebody stand up."

Annabelle Laws got up and stood there quietly.

"Thank you, young lady," Marvin said. "I can see you perfectly through my eyefinger. You have red hair and you're wearing a yellow shirt, correct?"

Everyone clapped.

"Somebody hold something up. Anything," Marvin said.

Terry Meaney reached into his pocket and pulled out a handkerchief. He waved it at the magician.

"What a handsome blue and green handkerchief," the man said. "But if you don't mind my saying so, it needs a good washing."

Terry scowled and sat down. The children laughed.

"Now I need a volunteer."

A girl on the other side of the hall stood up. Marvin turned and pointed at her with his finger.

"Yes, the young lady with the long blond

hair. Come up to the stage, please," he said, "and write something—anything—on the blackboard."

The girl meant to write, "I like apples," but she left the "e" out of "like" and spelled it "lik" instead.

"I lick apples too," Marvin said, pointing his finger at the blackboard. "But I prefer to lick ice cream."

Everyone laughed again, even some of the first graders who couldn't tell "lik" from "like." Well, almost everyone laughed. Emily just sat there with a big frown. Suddenly she stood up.

"Emily!" Janey whispered. "What are you doing?"

"All right, little girl," the magician said. "Do you want to write a message too?"

"Yes, I do, Mr. Marvin," Emily said.

"Just call me Magnificent," the man said. "Come on up here, don't be shy."

Emily wasn't shy at all. When she got to

the stage she went right up to the magician and reached for his hand.

"Hey! What do you think you're doing?" he said, snatching it away.

"I want to see your eyefinger," Emily said.

"Never mind about that, kid. Either write your message or sit down."

"Okay, I'll write a message," Emily said.

Emily got a piece of paper out of her pocket and wrote on it. She held it closely to her chest so he couldn't read it. Then she dropped it into the box that Marvin had pulled the rabbit out of.

"If you *really* have an eye on the end of your finger," Emily said, "put your hand in there and read what it says on the paper."

"Hey, what is this!" the man said. "Who's the magician around here? No little *girl*"—he said "girl" in a particularly nasty way—"is going to tell *me* what to do."

"Then I'm sorry but I don't believe you have a real eye on your finger," Emily said.

"Then how can I see you right now, smarty-pants?"

"You have a very thin blindfold and you can see straight through it," Emily answered. "That's my guess."

There was a murmur in the audience and the magician scowled behind his blindfold. He put his hand down in the box.

"It's dark in there," the magician said. "I won't be able to see what it says because it's too dark."

"No, it's not," Emily said. "If *you* put a note in the box, I'm sure I can read it with *my* eyefinger."

"Your what?" The man took off his blind-fold.

Emily pulled her hand out of her pocket and held it up. The children laughed.

"Who are you?" the magician whispered to Emily.

"My name is Emily," Emily said.

Marvin scribbled something on a piece of

paper and dropped it in the box. Emily put her hand in and looked at it through her eye-finger. It was dark in the box but she could still read the note. It said, "My teacher is a real stinker."

"Well?" Marvin asked with a smile. "Are you going to tell everyone what it says?"

"I *could*," said Emily, "but I won't. It's very rude."

"Yeah, tell me another one, kid. You're a fake and you know it."

"I'm not the one who's a fake," Emily said, "you are. And, besides, my teacher is not a stinker. She's a very nice person. So there."

Everyone burst out laughing again (except Ms. Plump) and Marvin went storming off stage. All the children stood up and clapped for Emily but she didn't even notice. She just walked out the door and back to her classroom.

In a few minutes the rest of Emily's class returned and Ms. Plump said to Emily, "I'm afraid you upset our magician."

"Well, he upset me too," Emily said.

"He says he wants to talk to you. Could you please go back to the auditorium?"

"Well, if he really wants me to," said Emily.

Emily pulled the curtain aside and there was Magnificent Marvin sitting with his head in his hands, looking sad.

"You're Emily Eyefinger, aren't you?" he said. "You're the one who was in the newspaper. You found that snake at the zoo."

"That's me," Emily said.

"Well, I got the idea of an eye on my finger from you."

"You did?"

"I sure did. I thought it would make my act more fun. And it did. Everyone loved it—but I didn't know you went to this school. I'm terribly sorry if I hurt your feelings. I'm not going to pretend I have an eyefinger anymore. I'll just go back to doing my usual magic tricks."

Emily thought about this for a moment

and then she said, "I'm sorry too. I'm sorry I ruined your magic show. I know that magicians don't do real magic—everything is a trick, really. Isn't that true?"

"Yes, of course, that's true."

"But I wasn't thinking. I got upset," Emily said, "because I was hoping that you were like me. I thought you had a real eye on your finger. I thought you could be my friend."

"And now you think I'm your enemy," the man said with a smile. "Why don't you just think of me as your *frenemy*—part friend and part enemy?"

Emily laughed.

"You say the funniest things," she said. "But I really don't mind if you pretend to have an eye on your finger. You keep on doing it in your show. It won't hurt my feelings one little bit. And I promise I won't tell anyone else that it's not real."

"That's very kind of you," the magician said. "Are you sure?"

"I'm sure."

"Hey, that's great! I've got an idea. How would you like to join my show? We could be partners. I can see it now — Magnificent Marvin and Amazing Emily's Super Spectacular Magic Show."

"Thank you very much," Emily said. "But I think I'm too young. I have to go to school and have lots of fun and grow up."

"Okay, but here's my telephone number in case you ever change your mind."

Emily took his telephone number. She knew that Marvin would turn out to be a real friend after all.

7

Emily Eyefinger, Spyfinger

One of Emily Eyefinger's most exciting adventures started one day when she came home from school. There with her parents were a man and a woman wearing long coats.

"These people are from SOFSOS, Emily," her father said. "They're on a very important mission and they need your help."

"What is 'softsoap'?" Emily asked.

"It's not *softsoap*—it's S-O-F-S-O-S: SOF-SOS," the woman said. "The Secret Organization for Spying on Spies. It's a very very strictly secret government organization and that's all we can tell you. We can't even tell you our real names. You may call me Ms. X and him Mr. Y. Will you help us?"

"If I can help you, I will," Emily said.

"Good," said Ms. X, smiling for a moment and then looking serious again. "First, we want you to meet King Crim of Slyvania."

"I see," said Emily.

"Not yet you don't," said Ms. X. "Come with us and we'll explain."

With this, Ms. X and Mr. Y took Emily to their big black car. They talked to her very quickly as they sped along.

"There's something fishy about this king fellow," Mr. Y explained.

"He *says* he's a king and he *says* he has come here on a special royal visit. He *says* he's from a country called the Kingdom of Slyvania," Ms. X added. "But, frankly, we're not sure he's telling the truth."

"We're a little bit suspicious," said Mr. Y.

"Partly because he looks like a sneaky guy," Ms. X said.

"And partly because there isn't any such country as—" Mr. Y started.

"Slyvania," Ms. X added.

"We think—" Mr. Y said.

"That he—" Ms. X said.

"Is a—" Mr. Y added.

"*Spy!*" Ms. X said, finishing Mr. Y's sentence.

Emily's neck was sore from looking back and forth from Ms. X to Mr. Y.

"What do you want *me* to do?" she asked. "If he's a spy, why don't you just catch him and put him in jail?"

"We're not absolutely and positively sure he's a spy," Mr. Y said. "And you can't put people in jail until you're absolutely and positively sure they're spies. Otherwise they get cranky."

"That's why we need you, Emily," Ms. X said.

"Well, I'm always happy to help," said Emily.

"He wears a big gold ring with a diamond on it on his right hand," Mr. Y said.

"We think there's some writing on the top of the ring next to the diamond," Ms. X added. "Don't forget to tell her that, Mr. Y."

"I was coming to that, Ms. X. We've tried to read the writing on the ring, Emily, but it's too small," said Mr. Y. "We think it might give us a clue about who he really is."

"We want you to have a good look at the writing with that . . . um . . . eye of yours," Ms. X said, pointing to Emily's eyefinger. "Then you can tell us what it says."

"How will I do that?" Emily asked.

"This afternoon he's going to meet some important people at a special reception with the mayor. We'd like you to be there too. Everyone will line up and shake hands with him the way people do when they meet kings and queens. Shake hands with your right hand but hold your left hand near the ring so you can read the writing. He won't notice a thing if you're clever about it."

"He might wonder why I'm there," Emily said. "I'm not an important person."

"She's got a point," Mr. Y said to Ms. X.

"I've been thinking about that," Ms. X said. "We'll tell him that you just won a prize for being the smartest little girl in the country. The prize is meeting him. He'll like that."

"But it's not true," Emily said. "I'm not the smartest little girl in the country. It would be lying."

"Don't worry about lying, Emily. We're allowed to lie," Mr. Y said. "It's part of our job."

Emily thought about it and then said, "There's another problem. Girls don't shake hands with kings, they curtsy. Men bow and girls and ladies curtsy. I read it in a book."

"The king doesn't care if people bow and curtsy," Ms. X said. "He says it's okay if everyone just shakes hands."

That afternoon Ms. X helped Emily get dressed in a beautiful gown that sparkled all over. She also had a wide hat with feathers on it. (They told her she'd have to give back the clothes after she met the king.)

She stood in a long line of important people who were all dressed up in expensive clothes. Finally King Crim came in and started shaking hands. Emily was nervous as she got her hand ready for the big shake. She took a few slow, deep breaths so she wouldn't be so nervous.

"And who, pray tell, is the young lady?" the king asked when it was Emily's turn.

"Emily Eyefinger, Your Highness," someone said, "the smartest little girl in the whole country."

A big smile spread like butter across King Crim's face.

"So you're the smartest little girl in the whole country," the king said, shaking her hand. "I'll bet you're not as smart as I am."

"I'm sure I'm not," Emily said, suddenly afraid that he'd ask her a hard question like *what is six times nine?*

The king gave a big laugh.

"I'll bet you thought I'd ask you a hard question," he said, still shaking hands.

"Yes, Your Majesty," Emily said, suddenly clutching his hand in both of hers.

"Well, I won't," the king said with a laugh, "because I can't think of any hard questions. My, what a strong handshake you have. Maybe you're the strongest little girl in the country too."

Emily gave a big sigh as the king moved on to the next person.

"*Pssst!*" Ms. X whispered when Emily came back. "What did the writing on the ring say?"

"It just said, 'to the king,' " Emily said. Ms. X and Mr. Y looked very unhappy until Emily added, "At least that's what it said on the top part."

"What do you mean?" Mr. Y asked.

"Well, there were words written on the bottom of the ring too."

"You could see them?" Ms. X asked.

"Only when I shook with both hands."

"Goodness! I think you *are* the smartest little girl in the country! What did the message say?"

"It said, 'To Arthur Crim, king of spies, hope you get the secrets. Best wishes from all your spy buddies.'"

"Aha!" Ms. X said, snapping her fingers. "He's Arthur Crim!"

"The famous spy?" Mr. Y asked.

"Exactly!" said Ms. X. "He steals secrets and then sells them to other countries. We were right. He isn't the king of anything. We've been trying to catch him for years but we didn't know what he looked like because he wears so many disguises."

"Let's arrest him now!" said Mr. Y.

"Not so fast," Ms. X said, holding him

back. "Let's find out how he steals the secrets and who he's working with. Then we'll arrest them all."

"But he'll see us following him. Spies always know when they're being followed."

Ms. X and Mr. Y scratched their heads and then their chins as they wondered what to do. They both looked at Emily.

"They would never suspect a little girl, would they?" Ms. X said with a grin. "Emily, you could be our own special secret agent."

"Secret agent?" said Emily. "That sounds exciting, but I think we had better talk it over with my parents."

8

Emily Eyefinger and the Case of the Missing Secrets

"**N**ow that your parents have given their okay," Ms. X said, "all you have to do is follow Arthur Crim to his hideout. Do just as we say and you'll be perfectly safe."

"But how can I follow this Arthur Crim?" asked Emily. "He knows what I look like."

"He may know what you look like now," Mr. Y said. "But even your best friend won't recognize you when we've finished."

With that, Ms. X and Mr. Y escorted

Emily to a secret room in a secret building. It was a room filled with disguises.

"First, we'll put this on," Ms. X said, putting a wig of short spiky hair on Emily's head.

"Then we'll put this in your mouth to make your face look fat," Mr. Y said, stuffing her cheeks full of cotton.

"You can wear these glasses. They just have plain glass in them. And put these false teeth in your mouth."

Emily got a shock when she looked in the mirror.

"That can't be me," she said.

"It is." Ms. X chuckled. "Now put on these jeans and this special blue spy coat quickly. The king will be leaving the meeting at any moment."

"What do I do?"

"You follow him, but not too close. When he gets to where he's going, telephone us. Here's some money for the phone call."

"Gosh, I feel just like Sarah Spy," said Emily, remembering the book she'd read called *Sarah Spy, Secret Agent*.

Ms. X and Mr. Y looked surprised.

"What do you mean?" they asked.

"Never mind," Emily said. "She's just someone in a book."

Emily followed King Crim along the street, stopping and looking in store windows whenever he turned around. When Emily thought he was getting suspicious, she walked ahead of him. All she had to do was secretly watch him with her eyefinger over her shoulder. He kept looking behind him. He never thought that he'd be followed by someone in *front* of him. He'd never heard of eyes on the ends of fingers.

Soon King Crim disappeared down a side street.

"Why, that sneaky guy," Emily thought. "If I turn and go down that street, he'll be watching. He'll know I'm following him."

Instead Emily ran around the block and got ahead of him again. When he got there, she was sitting on a bench holding up a newspaper, pretending to read it. Of course her eyefinger was watching him as he passed by.

Emily let him get ahead. She ducked behind a tree and took off the special blue spy coat. When she turned it inside out, it became a brown coat with white stripes. Emily hurried after him again.

When Emily thought King Crim was getting suspicious again, she went into a park and took a black floppy hat out of her pocket and put it on. Then she threw away the coat. Now she was wearing an orange jacket and a long dress. Once again Emily looked like a completely different person.

Across the city they went, through little streets and big streets and on buses and trains. She was ahead of him and she was behind him and she was beside him. Once she was even above him on a footbridge, her eyefinger peeking over the railing. All along the way she took off pieces of clothing and hid them. For a while she wore a purple sweater and then a checkered shirt. She turned the black hat inside out and it turned into a white sailor's hat. Then she had a pink shirt with red stripes. Finally she was down to a gray sweatshirt and jeans. She'd thrown away the hat.

"I hope he's getting close," thought Emily, "because I'm running out of disguises."

Just then King Crim turned into an alley and stopped. Emily followed. Now there was no one in the whole alley except Emily and King Crim. He watched as she walked by.

"Maybe he suspects me," Emily thought. "Or maybe his hideout is nearby and he's waiting until no one is looking before he goes in. Hmm, they didn't warn me about this."

Emily kept walking, looking back secretly with her eyefinger. But King Crim didn't budge. She turned the corner and quickly peeked back around the edge of the building with her eyefinger. But it was too late. He was gone.

"Oh, rats!" said Emily. "He tricked me. What am I going to tell Ms. X and Mr. Y?"

Emily dashed back to where King Crim had been. On one side of the alley was a dirty old building with broken windows.

"I wonder if he went back the way we came?" Emily thought. "No, I'll bet he went into this building. I could call Ms. X and Mr. Y, but maybe I'd better have a look — just to be sure he's in there."

Up the fire escape Emily crept, peering through windows at the dusty darkness inside. Slowly she opened a window and climbed in.

"Gotcha!" a voice yelled and four arms reached out and grabbed her.

A light went on. Two men were holding her — a tall man and a short man. Standing in front of her was King Crim.

"And who might you be?" King Crim said, pulling off Emily's wig and glasses. "My goodness, it's you, the smartest little girl in the country! What happened to your teeth? They look terrible. And your face! You don't have the mumps, do you?"

"I'm really not sick," Emily said, taking the cotton and false teeth out of her mouth. "See?"

"You're a very naughty girl for coming in here," King Crim said. "You must have been following me. And if you were, you certainly were good at it. I didn't suspect a thing until I saw you coming up the fire escape."

Emily didn't say anything.

"Well, then," King Crim went on, "we'll just have to keep you here till we make our getaway. Tie her up, boys. Use a lot of knots because she's the smartest girl in the country. Ha ha ha ha ha ha ha."

The *ha ha ha*'s were not funny *ha ha ha*'s but scary *ha ha ha*'s. They made a shiver go up Emily's spine. The two men tied her hands behind her back. She kept her hands closed so they couldn't see her eyefinger. Finally they tied her to a chair.

"Your plan worked perfectly, boss," the tall man said to King Crim. "While all those important government people were meeting you, we broke into their offices and stole a whole bagful of secrets."

"Yeah. Heh, heh, heh," said the short one. He opened a big bag and showed King Crim all the papers.

"Good work," said King Crim. "We'll catch a plane out of the country tonight. Tomorrow we'll sell the secrets and be rich. Did you bring the disguises?"

"Sure, boss," said the tall one, opening a suitcase.

Emily opened her hand and looked with her eyefinger at the knots that tied her wrists. One by one she started undoing them secretly as the three men put on false beards and sunglasses.

"Ha ha ha ha," Crim laughed, pointing to the other two. "You both look silly."

"You look pretty silly yourself," the tall one said. "Hurry up. Let's get out of here."

King Crim grabbed the bag of secrets and started out the door after the two men. As soon as the men were out the door Emily had her hands free. She quickly jumped through the window and ran down the fire escape to the street. Driving along the street in their big black car were secret agents Ms. X and Mr. Y.

"Thank heavens we've found you," Ms. X said, stopping the car. "We were following you but you disappeared."

"Never mind about me," Emily said. "King Crim and two of his men will be coming out that door at any minute. They have a whole bagful of stolen secrets!"

Just then King Crim and his men burst through the doorway.

"Hold it right there, Arthur Crim!" Ms. X yelled. "We know who you are!"

"That goes for you too!" Mr. Y yelled as he grabbed the tall man and the short man by their coat collars.

King Crim took one look at the two agents and broke into a run with Ms. X hot on his heels. Before he could round the corner, she took a flying leap and grabbed him around the legs, bringing him down with a terrible crash. Then she handcuffed his hands behind his back.

"Crime never pays, mister smart guy," she said. "When are you going to learn that?"

Before the agents from SOFSOS took the three spies off to jail, King Crim turned to Emily and asked, "How did you get away so fast?"

Emily wasn't going to tell him about her eyefinger.

"Don't you remember?" Emily said. "I'm the smartest little girl in the country."

Ms. X and Mr. Y laughed, and that was how Emily Eyefinger solved the Case of the Missing Secrets.

Emily was given a special secret spying award, which, of course, she had to keep secret from everyone except her parents.

"We're very proud of you," her father said. "Now do you still want your eyefinger or would you like the doctor to take it off?"

"Well," said Emily, "on the one hand I like it. But on the other hand I don't."

They all had a good laugh and that was the end of that.

About the author

Although he was born in Boston, Duncan Ball has spent much of his life abroad, and now lives in Sydney, Australia, with his wife, Jill, a violist. He is the author of many books for children, including *Emily Eyefinger* and *Jeremy's Tail*, which *Kirkus Reviews* praised as an "outrageously tall tale" that "will keep young audiences giggling."

Duncan Ball loves to travel, take photographs, and climb mountains, which no doubt contributes to his heightened sense of the ridiculous.

Emily Eyefinger, Secret Agent is a companion to *Emily Eyefinger*.

About the illustrator

George Ulrich lives in Marblehead, Massachusetts. He has illustrated many books for young readers, including *The Million Dollar Potato* by Louis Phillips and *Emily Eyefinger*.

NCC